The Winds of Time

Other Books by James H. Schmitz

The Demon Breed
The Universe Against Her
The Witches of Karres

The Winds of Time

James H. Schmitz

ÆGYPAN PRESS

This text from *Analog*, September, 1962.

Special thanks to Greg Weeks, Stephen Blundell and
the Online Distributed Proofreading Team (which can
be found at http://www.pgdp.net).

The Winds of Time
A publication of
ÆGYPAN PRESS

www.aegypan.com

He contracted for a charter trip — but the man who hired his spacer wasn't quite a man, it turned out — and he wanted more than service!

Gefty Rammer came along the narrow passages between the *Silver Queen's* control compartment and the staterooms, trying to exchange the haggard look on his face for one of competent self-assurance. There was nothing to gain by letting his two passengers suspect that during the past few minutes their pilot, the owner of Rammer Spacelines, had been a bare step away from plain and fancy gibbering.

He opened the door to Mr. Maulbow's stateroom and went inside. Mr. Maulbow, face very pale, eyes closed, lay on his back on the couch, still unconscious. He'd been knocked out when some unknown forces suddenly started batting the *Silver Queen's* turnip-shape around as the *Queen* had never been batted before in her eighteen years of spacefaring. Kerim Ruse, Maulbow's secretary, knelt beside her employer, checking his pulse. She looked anxiously up at Gefty.

"What did you find out?" she asked in a voice that was not very steady.

Gefty shrugged. "Nothing definite as yet. The ship hasn't been damaged — she's a tough tub. That's one good point. Otherwise . . . well, I climbed into a suit and took a look out the escape hatch. And I saw the same thing there that the screens show. Whatever that is."

"You've no idea then of what's happened to us, or where we are?" Miss Ruse persisted. She was a rather small girl with large, beautiful grey eyes and thick blue-black hair. At the moment, she was barefoot and in a sleeping outfit which consisted of something soft wrapped around her top, soft and floppy trousers below. The black hair was tousled and she looked around fifteen. She'd been asleep in her state-room when something smacked the *Queen*, and she was sensible enough then not to climb out of the bunk's safety field until the ship finally stopped shuddering and bucking about. That made her the only one of the three persons aboard who had collected no bruises. She was scared, of course, but taking the situation very well.

Gefty said carefully, "There're a number of possibilities. It's obvious that the *Queen* has been knocked out of normspace, and it may take some time to find out how to get her back there. But the main thing is that the ship's intact. So far, it doesn't look too bad."

Miss Ruse seemed somewhat reassured. Gefty could hardly have said the same for himself. He was a qualified normspace and subspace pilot. He had put in a hitch with the Federation Navy, and for the past eight years he'd been ferrying his own two ships about the Hub and not infrequently beyond the Federation's space territories, but he had never heard of a situation like this. What he saw in the viewscreens when the ship steadied enough to let him pick himself off the instrument room floor, and again, a few minutes later and with much more immediacy, from the escape hatch, made no sense — seemed simply to have no meaning. The pressure meters said there was a vacuum outside the *Queen's* skin. That vacuum was dark, even pitch-black but here and there came momentary suggestions of vague light and color. Occasional pinpricks of brightness showed and were gone. And there had been one startling phenomenon like a distant, giant explosion, a sudden pallid glare in the dark, which appeared far ahead of the *Queen* and, for the instant it remained in sight, seemed to be rushing directly towards them. It had given Gefty the feeling that the ship itself was plowing at high speed through this eerie medium. But he had cut the *Queen's* drives to the merest idling pulse as soon as he staggered back to the control console and got his first look at the screens, so it must have been the light that had moved.

But such details were best not discussed with a passenger. Kerim Ruse would be arriving at enough disquieting speculations on her own; the less he told her, the better. There was the matter of the ship's location instruments. The only set Gefty had been able to obtain any reading on were the direction indicators. And what they appeared to indicate was that the *Silver Queen* was turning on a new heading something like twenty times a second.

Gefty asked, "Has Mr. Maulbow shown any signs of waking up?"

Kerim shook her head. "His breathing and pulse seem all right, and that bump on his head doesn't look really bad, but he hasn't moved at all. Can you think of anything else we might do for him, Gefty?"

"Not at the moment," Gefty said. "He hasn't broken any bones. We'll see how he feels when he comes out of it." He was wondering about Mr. Maulbow and the fact that this charter had showed some unusual features from the beginning.

Kerim was a friendly sort of girl; they'd got to calling each other by their first names within a day or two after the trip started. But after that, she seemed to be avoiding him; and Gefty guessed that Maulbow had spoken to her, probably to make sure that Kerim didn't let any of her employer's secrets slip out.

Maulbow himself was as aloof and taciturn a client as Rammer Spacelines ever had picked up. A lean, blond character of indeterminate age, with pale eyes, hard mouth. Why he had selected a bulky semifreighter like the *Queen* for a mineralogical survey jaunt to a lifeless little sun system far beyond the outposts of civilization was a point he didn't discuss. Gefty, needing the charter money, had restrained his curiosity. If Maulbow wanted only a pilot and preferred to do all the rest of the work himself, that was certainly Maulbow's affair. And if he happened to be up to something illegal — though it was difficult to imagine what — Customs would nail him when they got back to the Hub.

But those facts looked a little different now.

Gefty scratched his chin, inquired, "Do you happen to know where Mr. Maulbow keeps the keys to the storage vault?"

Kerim looked startled. "Why, no! I couldn't permit you to take the keys anyway while he . . . while he's unconscious! You know that."

Gefty grunted. "Any idea of what he has locked up in the vault?"

"You shouldn't ask me —" Her eyes widened. "Why, that couldn't possibly have anything to do with what's happened!"

He might, Gefty thought, have reassured her a little too much. He said, "I wouldn't know. But I don't want to just sit here and wonder about it until Maulbow wakes up. Until we're back in normspace, we'd better not miss any bets. Because one thing's sure — if this has happened to anybody else, they didn't turn up again to report it. You see?"

Kerim apparently did. She went pale, then said hesitantly, "Well . . . the sealed cases Mr. Maulbow brought out from the Hub with him had some very expensive instruments in them. That's all I know. He's always trusted me not to pry into his business anymore than my secretarial duties required, and of course I haven't."

"You don't know then what it was he brought up from that moon a few hours ago — those two big cases he stowed away in the vault?"

"No, I don't, Gefty. You see, he hasn't told me what the purpose of this trip is. I only know that it's a matter of great importance to him." Kerim paused, added, "From the careful manner Mr. Maulbow handled the cases with the cranes, I had the impression that whatever was inside them must be quite heavy."

"I noticed that," Gefty said. It wasn't much help. "Well, I'll tell *you* something now," he went on. "I let your boss keep both sets of keys to the storage vault because he insisted on it when he signed the charter. What I didn't tell him was that I could make up a duplicate set any time in around half an hour."

"Oh! Have you — ?"

"Not yet. But I intend to take a look at what Mr. Maulbow's got in that vault now, with or without his consent. You'd better run along and get dressed while I take him up to the instrument room."

"Why move him?" Kerim asked.

"The instrument room's got an overall safety field. I've turned it on now, and if something starts banging us around again, the room will be the safest place on the ship. I'll bring his personal luggage up too, and you can start looking through it for the keys. You may find them before I get a new set made. Or he may wake up and tell us where they are."

Kerim Ruse gave her employer a dubious glance, then nodded, said, "I imagine you're right, Gefty," and pattered hurriedly out of the stateroom. A few minutes later, she arrived, fully dressed, in the instrument room. Gefty looked around from the table-shelf where he had laid out his tools, and said, "He hasn't stirred. His suitcases are over there. I've unlocked them."

Kerim gazed at what showed in the screens about the control console and shivered slightly. She said, "I was thinking, Gefty . . . isn't there something they call Space Three?"

"Sure. Pseudospace. But that isn't where we are. There're some special-built Navy tubs that can operate in that stuff if they don't stay too long. A ship like the *Queen* . . . well, you and I and everything else in here would be frozen solid by now if we'd got sucked somehow into Space Three."

"I see," Kerim said uncomfortably. Gefty heard her move over to the suitcases. After a moment, she asked, "What do the vault keys look like?"

"You can't miss them if he's just thrown them in there. They're over six inches long. What kind of a guy is this Maulbow? A scientist?"

"I couldn't say, Gefty. He's never referred to himself as a scientist. I've had this job a year and a half. Mr. Maulbow is a very considerate employer . . . one of the nicest men I've known, really. But it was simply understood that I should ask no questions about the business beyond what I actually needed to know for my work."

"What's the business called?"

"Maulbow Engineering."

"Big help," Gefty observed, somewhat sourly. "Those instruments he brought along . . . he build those himself?"

"No, but I think he designed some of them — probably most of them. The companies he had doing the actual work appeared to have a terrible time getting everything exactly the way Mr. Maulbow wanted it — There's nothing that looks like a set of keys in those first two suitcases, Gefty."

"Well," Gefty said, "if you don't find them in the others, you might start thumping around to see if he's got secret compartments in his luggage somewhere."

"I do wish," Kerim Ruse said uneasily, "that Mr. Maulbow would regain consciousness. It seems so . . . so underhanded to be doing these things behind his back!"

Gefty grunted noncommittally. He wasn't at all certain by now that he wanted his secretive client to wake up before he'd checked on the contents of the *Queen's* storage vault.

*F*ifteen minutes later, Gefty Rammer was climbing down to the storage deck in the *Queen's* broad stern, the newly fashioned set of vault keys clanking heavily in his coat pocket. Kerim had remained with her employer who was getting back his color but still hadn't opened his eyes. She hadn't found the original keys. Gefty wasn't sure she'd tried too hard, though she seemed to realize the seriousness of the situation now. But her loyalty to Mr. Maulbow could make no further difference, and she probably felt more comfortable for it.

Lights went on automatically in the wide passage leading from the cargo lock to the vault as Gefty turned into it. His steps echoed between the steel bulkheads on either side. He paused a moment before the big circular vault doors, listening to the purr of the *Queen's* idling engines in the next compartment. The familiar sound was somehow reassuring. He inserted the first key, turned it over twice, drew it out again and pressed one of the buttons in the control panel beside the door. The heavy slab of steel moved sideways with a soft, hissing sound, vanished into the wall. Gefty slid the other key into the lock of the inner door. A few seconds later, the vault entrance lay open before him.

He stood still again, wrinkling his nose. The area ahead was only dimly illuminated — the shaking-up the *Queen* had undergone had disturbed the lighting system here. And what was that odor? Rather sharp, unpleasant; it might have been spilled ammonia. Gefty stepped through the door into the wide, short entrance passage beyond it, turned to the right and peered about in the semidarkness of the vault.

Two great steel cases — the ones Maulbow had taken down to an airless moon surface, loaded up with something and brought back to the *Queen* — were jammed awkwardly into a corner, in a manner which suggested they'd slid into it when the ship was being knocked around. One of them was open and appeared to be empty. Gefty wasn't sure of the other. In the dimness beside them lay the loose coils of some very thick, dark cable — And standing near the center of the floor was a thing that at once riveted his attention on it completely. He sucked his breath in softly, feeling chilled.

He realized he hadn't really believed his own hunch. But, of course, if it hadn't been an unheard-of outside force that plucked the *Queen* out of normspace and threw her into this elsewhere, then it must be something Maulbow had put on board. And that something had to be a machine of some kind —

It was.

About it he could make out a thin gleaming of wires — a jury-rigged safety field. Within the flimsy-looking protective cage was a double bank of instruments, some of them alive with the flicker and glow of lights. Those must be the very expensive and difficult-to-build items Maulbow had brought out from the Hub. Beside them stood the machine, squat and ponderous. In the vague light, it looked misshaped and discolored. A piece of equipment that had taken a bad beating of some kind. But it was functioning. As he stared, intermittent bursts of clicking noises rose from it, like the staccato of irregular gunfire.

For a moment, questions raced in disorder through his mind. What was it? Why had it been on that moon? Part of another ship, wrecked now . . . a ship that had been at home *here?* Was it some sort of drive?

Maulbow must know. He'd known enough to design the instruments required to bring the battered monster back to life. On the other hand, he had not foreseen in all detail what could happen once the thing was in operation, because the *Queen's* sudden buck-jumping act had surprised him and knocked him out.

The first step, in any event, was to get Maulbow awake now. To tamper with a device like this, before learning as much as one could about it, would be lunatic foolhardiness. It looked like too good a bet that the next serious mistake made by anybody would finish them all —

Perhaps it was only because Gefty's nerves were on edge that he grew aware at that point in his reflections of two minor signals from his senses. One was that the smell of ammonia, which he had almost stopped noticing, was becoming appreciably stronger. The other was the faintest of sounds — a whispering suggestion of motion somewhere behind him. But here in the storage vault nothing should have moved, and Gefty's muscles were tensing as his head came around. Almost in the same instant, he flung himself wildly to one side, stumbling and regaining his balance as something big and dark slapped heavily down on the floor at the point where he had stood. Then he was darting up through the entrance passage, turning, and knocking down the lock switches on the outside door panel.

It came flowing around the corner of the passage behind him as the vault doors began to slide together. He was aware mainly of swift, smooth, oiling motion like that of a big snake; then, for a fraction of a second, a strip of brighter light from the outside passage showed a long, heavy wedge of a head, a green metal-glint of staring eyes.

The doors closed silently into their frames and locked. The thing was inside. But it was almost a minute then before Gefty could control his shaking legs enough to start moving back towards the main deck. In the half-dark of the vault, it had looked like a big coiled cable lying next to the packing cases. Like Maulbow, it might have been battered around and knocked out during the recent disturbance; and when it recovered, it had found Gefty in the vault with it. But it might also have been awake all the while, waiting cunningly until Gefty's attention seemed fixed elsewhere before launching its attack. It was big enough to have flattened him and smashed every bone in his body if the stroke had landed.

Some kind of guard animal — a snake-like watchdog? What other connection could it have with the mystery machine? Perhaps Maulbow had intended to leave it confined in one of the cases, and it had broken loose —

Too many questions by now, Gefty thought. But Maulbow had the answers.

*H*e was hurrying up the main deck's central passage when Maulbow's voice addressed him sharply from a door he'd just passed.

"Stop right there, Rammer! Don't dare to move! I —"

The voice ended on a note of surprise. Gefty's reaction had not been too rational, but it was prompt. Maulbow's tone and phrasing implied he was armed. Gefty wasn't, but he kept a gun in the instrument room for emergencies. He'd been through a whole series of unnerving experiences, winding up with being shagged out of his storage vault by something that stank of ammonia and looked like a giant snake. To have one of the *Queen's* passengers order him to stand where he was topped it off. Every other consideration was swept aside by a great urge to get his hands on his gun.

He glanced back, saw Maulbow coming out of the half-opened door, something like a twenty-inch, thin, white rod in one hand. Then Gefty went bounding on along the passage, hunched forward and zigzagging from wall to wall to give Maulbow — if the thing he held was a weapon and he actually intended to use it — as small and erratic a target as possible.

Maulbow shouted angrily behind him. Then, as Gefty came up to the next cross-passage, a line of white fire seared through the air across his shoulders and smashed off the passage wall.

With that, he was around the corner, and boiling mad. He had no great liking for gunfire, but it didn't shake him like the silently attacking beast in the dark storage had done. He reached the deserted instrument room not many seconds later, had his gun out and cocked, and was faced back towards the passage by which he had entered. Maulbow, if he had pursued without hesitation, should be arriving by now. But the passage stayed quiet. Gefty couldn't see into it from where he stood. He waited, trying to steady his breathing, wondering where Kerim Ruse was and what had got into Maulbow. After a moment, without taking his eyes from the passage entrance, he reached into the wall closet from which he had taken the gun and fished out another souvenir of his active service days, a thin-bladed knife in a slip-sheath. Gefty worked the fastenings of the sheath over his left wrist and up his forearm under his coat, tested the release to make sure it was functioning, and shook his coat sleeve back into place.

The passage was still quiet. Gefty moved softly over to one of the chairs, took a small cushion from it and pitched it out in front of the entrance.

There was a hiss. The cushion turned in midair into a puff of bright white fire. Gefty aimed his gun high at the far passage wall just beyond the entrance and pulled the trigger. It was a projectile gun. He heard the slug screech off the slick plastic bulkhead and go slamming down the passage. Somebody out there made a startled, incoherent noise. But not the kind of a noise a man makes when he's just been hit.

"If you come in here armed," Gefty called, "I'll blow your head off. Want to stop this nonsense now?"

There was a moment's silence. Then Maulbow's voice replied shakily from the passage. He seemed to be standing about twenty feet back from the room.

"If you'll end your thoughtless attempts at interference, Rammer," he said, "there will be no trouble." He was speaking with the restraint of a man who is in a state of cold fury. "You're endangering us all. You must realize that you have no understanding of what you are doing."

Well, the last could be true enough. "We'll talk about it," Gefty said without friend-liness. "I haven't done anything yet, but I'm not just handing the ship over to you. And what have you done with Miss Ruse?"

Maulbow hesitated again. "She's in the map room," he said then. "I . . . it was necessary to restrict her movements for a while. But you might as well let her out now. We must reach an agreement without loss of time."

Gefty glanced over his shoulder at the small closed door of the map room. There was no lock on the door, and he had heard no sound from inside; this might be some trick. But it wouldn't take long to find out. He backed up to the wall, pushed the door open and looked inside.

Kerim was there, sitting on a chair in one corner of the tiny room. The reason she hadn't made any noise became clear. She and the chair were covered by a rather closely fitting sack of transparent, glistening fabric. She stared out through it despairingly at Gefty, her lips moving urgently. But no sound came from the sack.

Gefty called angrily, "Maulbow —"

"Don't excite yourself, Rammer." There was a suggestion of what might be contempt in Maulbow's tone now. "The girl hasn't been harmed. She can breathe easily through the restrainer. And you can remove it by pulling at the material from outside."

Gefty's mouth tightened. "I'll keep my gun on the passage while I do it —"

Maulbow didn't answer. Gefty edged back into the map room, tentatively grasped the transparent stuff above Kerim's shoulder. To his surprise, it parted like wet tissue. He pulled sharply, and in a moment Kerim came peeling herself out of it, her face tear-stained, working desperately with hands, elbows and shoulders.

"Gefty," she gasped, "he . . . Mr. Maulbow —"

"He's out in the passage there," Gefty
said. "He can hear you." His glance shifted for
an instant to the wall where a second of the
shroudlike transparencies was hanging. And
who could that have been intended for, he
thought, but Gefty Rammer? He added, "We've
had a little trouble."

"Oh!" She looked out of the room towards the passage, then at the gun in Gefty's
hand, then up at his face.

"Maulbow," Gefty went on, speaking dis-
tinctly enough to make sure Maulbow heard,
"has a gun, too. He'll stay there in the passage
and we'll stay in the instrument room until we
agree on what should be done. He's responsible
for what's happened and seems to know where
we are."

He looked at Kerim's frightened eyes,
dropped his voice to a whisper. "Don't let this
worry you too much. I haven't found out just
what he's up to, but so far his tricks have pretty

much backfired. He was counting on taking us both by surprise, for one thing. That didn't work, so now he'd like us to co-operate."

"Are you going to?"

Gefty shrugged. "Depends on what he has in mind. I'm just interested in getting us out of this alive. Let's hear what Maulbow has to say —"

Some minutes later Gefty was trying to decide whether it was taking a worse risk to believe what Maulbow said than to keep things stalled on the chance that he was lying.

Kerim Ruse, perched stiffly erect on the edge of a chair, eyes big and round, face almost colorless, apparently believed Maulbow and was wishing she didn't. There was, of course, some supporting evidence . . . primarily the improbable appearance of their surroundings. The pencil-thin fire-spouter and the sleazy-looking "restrainer" had a sufficiently unfamiliar air to go with Maulbow's story; but as far as Gefty

knew, either of them could have been manufac-
tured in the Hub.

Then there was the janandra — the big,
snakish thing in the storage which Maulbow
had brought back up from the moon along with
the battered machine. It had been, he said, his
shipboard companion on another voyage. It
wasn't ordinarily aggressive — Gefty's sudden
appearance in the vault must have startled it into
making an attack. It was not exactly a pet. There
was a psychological relationship between it and
Maulbow which Maulbow would not attempt
to explain because Gefty and Kerim would be
unable to grasp its significance. The janandra
was essential, in this unexplained manner, to his
well-being.

That item was almost curious enough to
seem to substantiate his other statements; but it
didn't really prove anything. The only point
Gefty didn't question in the least was that they
were in a bad spot which might be getting worse
rapidly. His gaze shifted back to the screens.
What he saw out there, surrounding the ship,

was, according to Maulbow, an illusion of space created by the time flow in which they were moving.

Also according to Maulbow, there was a race of the future, human in appearance, with machines to sail the current of time through the universe — to run and tack with the winds of time, dipping in and out of the normspace of distant periods and galaxies as they chose. Maulbow, one of the explorers, had met disaster a million light-years from the home of his kind, centuries behind them, his vehicle wrecked on an airless moon with damaged control unit and shattered instruments. He had made his way to a human civilization to obtain the equipment he needed, and returned at last with the *Silver Queen* to where the time-sailer lay buried.

Gefty's lip curled. No, he wasn't buying all that just yet — but if Maulbow was *not* lying, then the unseen stars were racing past, the mass of the galaxy beginning to slide by, eventually to be lost forever beyond a black distance no space drive could span. The matter simply had to be settled quickly. But Maulbow was also strained and impatient, and if his impatience could be increased a little more, he might start telling the things that really mattered, the things Gefty had to know. Gefty asked slowly, as if hesitant to commit himself, "Why did you bring us along?"

The voice from the passage snapped, "Because my resources were nearly exhausted, Rammer! I couldn't obtain a new ship. Therefore I chartered yours; and you came with it. As for Miss Ruse — in spite of every precaution, my activities may have aroused suspicion and curiosity among your people. When I disappeared, Miss Ruse might have been questioned. I couldn't risk being followed to the wreck of the sailer, so I took her with me. And what does that mean against what I have offered you? The greatest adventure — followed, I give you my solemn word, by a safe return to your own place and time, and the most generous compensations for any inconvenience you may have suffered!"

Kerim, looking up at Gefty, shook her head violently. Gefty said, "We find it difficult to take you on trust now, Maulbow. Why do you want to get into the instrument room?"

Maulbow was silent for some seconds. Then he said, "As I told you, this ship would not have been buffeted about during the moments of transfer if the control unit were operating with complete efficiency. Certain adjustments will have to be made in the unit, and this should be done promptly."

"Where do the ship instruments come in?" Gefty asked.

"I can determine the nature of the problem from them. When I was . . . stranded . . . the unit was seriously damaged. My recent repairs were necessarily hasty. I —"

"What caused the crack-up?"

Maulbow said, tone taut with impatience, "Certain sections of the Great Current are infested with dangerous forces. I shall not attempt to describe them . . ."

"I wouldn't get it?"

"I don't pretend to understand them very well myself, Rammer. They are not life but show characteristics of life — even of intelligent life. If you can imagine radiant energy being capable of conscious hostility. . . ."

There was a chill at the back of Gefty's neck. "A big, fast-moving light?"

"Yes!" Sharp concern showed suddenly in the voice from the passage. "You . . . when did you see that?"

Gefty glanced at the screens. "Twice since you've been talking. And once before — immediately after we got tumbled around."

"Then we can waste no more time, Rammer. Those forces are sensitive to the fluctuations of the control unit. If they were close enough to be seen, they're aware the ship is here. They were attempting to locate it."

"What could they do?"

Maulbow said, "A single attack was enough to put the control unit out of operation in my sailer. The Great Current then rejected us instantly. A ship of this size might afford more protection, which is the reason I chose it. But if the control unit is not adjusted immediately to enable it to take us out of this section, the attacks will continue until the ship — and we — have been destroyed."

Gefty drew a deep breath. "There's another solution to that problem, Maulbow. Miss Ruse and I prefer it. And if you meant what you said — that you'd see to it we got back eventually — you shouldn't object either."

The voice asked sharply, "What do you mean?"

Gefty said, "Shut the control unit off. From what you were saying, that throws us automatically back into normspace, while we're still close enough to the Hub. You'll find plenty of people there who'll stake you to a trip to the future if they can go along and are convinced they'll return. Miss Ruse and I don't happen to be that adventurous."

There was silence from the passage. Gefty added, "Take your time to make up your mind about it, if you want to. I don't like the idea of those lights hitting us, but neither do you. And I think I can wait this out as well as you can. . . ."

The silence stretched out. Presently Gefty said, "If you do accept, slide that fire-shooting device of yours into the room before you show up. We don't want accidents."

He paused again. Kerim was chewing her lips, hands clenched into small fists in her lap. Then Maulbow answered, voice flat and expressionless now.

"The worst thing we can do at present," he said, "is to prolong a dispute about possible courses of action. If I disarm, will you lay aside your gun?"

"Yes."

"Then I accept your conditions, disappointing as they are."

He was silent. After a moment, Gefty heard the white rod clatter lightly along the floor of the passage. It struck the passage wall, spun off it, and rolled into the instrument room, coming to rest a few feet away from him. Gefty hesitated, picked it up and laid it on the wall table. He placed his own gun beside it, moved a dozen steps away. Kerim's eyes followed him anxiously.

"Gefty," she whispered, "he might . . ."

Gefty looked at her, formed the words "It's all right" with his mouth and called, "Guns have been put aside, Maulbow. Come on in, and let's keep it peaceable."

He waited, arms hanging loosely at his side, heart beating heavily, as quick footsteps came up the passage. Maulbow appeared in the entrance, glanced at Gefty and Kerim, then about the room. His gaze rested for a moment on the wall table, shifted back to Gefty. Maulbow came on into the room, turning towards Gefty, mouth twisting.

He said softly, "It is not our practice, Rammer, to share the secrets of the Great Current with other races. I hadn't foreseen that you might become a dangerous nuisance. But now —"

His right hand began to lift, half closed about some small golden instrument. Gefty's left arm moved back and quickly forwards.

The service knife slid out of its sheath and up from his palm as an arrow of smoky blackness burst from the thing in Maulbow's hand. The blackness came racing with a thin, snarling noise across the floor towards Gefty's feet. The knife flashed above it, turning, and stood hilt-deep in Maulbow's chest.

Gefty returned a few minutes later from the forward cabin which served as the *Queen's* sick bay, and said to Kerim, "He's still alive, though I don't know why. He may even recover. He's full of anesthetic, and that should keep him quiet till we're back in normspace. Then I'll see what we can do for him."

Kerim had lost some of her white, shocked look while he was gone. "You knew he would try to kill you?" she asked shakily.

"Suspected he had it in mind — he gave in too quick. But I thought I'd have a chance to take any gadget he was hiding away from him first. I was wrong about that. Now we'd better move fast . . ."

He switched the emergency check panel back on, glanced over the familiar patterns of lights and numbers. A few minor damage spots were indicated, but the ship was still fully operational. One minor damage spot which did not appear on the panel was now to be found in the instrument room itself, in the corner on which the door of the map room opened. The door, the adjoining bulkheads and section of flooring were scarred, blackened, and as assortedly malodorous as burned things tend to become. That was where Gefty had stood when Maulbow entered the room, and if he had remained there an instant after letting go of the knife, he would have been in very much worse condition than the essentially fireproof furnishings.

Both Maulbow's weapons — the white rod lying innocently on the wall table and the round, golden device which had dropped from his hand spitting darts of smoking blackness — had blasted unnervingly away into that area for almost thirty seconds after Maulbow was down and twisting about on the floor. Then he went limp and the firing instantly stopped. Apparently, Maulbow's control of them had ended as he lost consciousness.

It seemed fortunate that the sick bay cabin's emergency treatment accessories, gentle as their action was, might have been designed for the specific purpose of keeping the most violent of prisoners immobilized — let alone one with a terrible knife wound in him. At the angle along which the knife had driven in and up below the ribs, an ordinary man would have been dead in seconds. But it was very evident now that Maulbow was no ordinary man, and even after the eerie weapons had been pitched out of the ship through the instrument room's disposal tube, Gefty couldn't rid himself of an uncomfortable suspicion that he wasn't done with Maulbow yet — wouldn't be done with him, in fact, until one or the other of them was dead.

He said to Kerim, "I thought the machine Maulbow set up in the storage vault would turn out to be some drive engine, but apparently it has an entirely different function. He connected it with the instruments he had made in the Hub, and together they form what he calls a control unit. The emergency panel would show if the unit were drawing juice from the ship. It isn't, and I don't know what powers it. But we do know now that the control unit is holding us in the time current, and it will go on holding us there as long as it's in operation.

"If we could shut it off, the *Queen* would be 'rejected' by the current, like Maulbow's sailer was. In other words, we'd get knocked back into normspace — which is what we want. And we want it to happen as soon as possible because, if Maulbow was telling the truth on that point, every minute that passes here is taking us farther away from the Hub, and farther from our own time towards his."

Kerim nodded, eyes intent on his face.

"Now I can't just go down there and start slapping switches around on the thing," Gefty went on. "He said it wasn't working right, and even if it were, I couldn't tell what would happen. But it doesn't seem to connect up with any ship systems — it just seems to be holding us in a field of its own. So I should be able to move the whole unit into the cargo lock and eject it from there. If we shift the *Queen* outside its field, that should have the same effect as shutting the control unit off. It should throw us back into normspace."

Kerim nodded again. "What about Mr. Maulbow's janandra animal?"

Gefty shrugged. "Depends on the mood I find it in. He said it wasn't usually aggressive.

Maybe it isn't. I'll get into a spacesuit for protection and break out some of the mining equipment to move it along with. If I can maneuver it into an empty compartment where it will be out of the . . ."

*H*e broke off, expression changing, eyes fastened on the emergency panel. Then he turned hurriedly, reached across the side of the console for the intership airseal controls. Kerim asked apprehensively, "What's the matter, Gefty?"

"Wish I knew . . . exactly." Gefty indicated the emergency panel. "Little red light there, on the storage deck section — it wasn't showing a minute ago. It means that the vault doors have been opened since then."

He saw the same half-superstitious fear appear in her face that had touched him. "You think *he* did it?"

"I don't know." Maulbow's control of the guns had seemed uncanny enough. But that was a different matter. The guns were a product of his own time and science. But the vault door mechanisms? There might have been sufficient opportunity for Maulbow to study them and alter them, for some purpose of his own, since he'd come aboard. . . .

"I've got the ship compartments and decks sealed off from each other now," Gefty said slowly. "The only connecting points from one to the other are personnel hatches — they're small air locks. So the janandra's confined to the storage deck. If it's come out of the vault, it might be a nuisance until I can get equipment to handle it. But that isn't too serious. The spacesuits are on the second deck, and I'll get into one before I go on to the storage. You wait here a moment, I'll look in on Maulbow again before I start."

If Maulbow wasn't still unconscious, he was doing a good job of feigning it. Gefty looked at the pale, lax face, the half-shut eyes, shook his head and left the cabin, locking it behind him. It mightn't be Maulbow's doing, but having the big snake loose in the storage could, in fact, make things extremely awkward now. He didn't think his gun would make much impression on anything of that size, and while several of the ship's mining tools could be employed as very effective close-range weapons, they happened, unfortunately, to be stored away on the same deck.

He found Kerim standing in the center of the instrument room, waiting for him.

"Gefty," she said, "do you notice anything? An odd sort of smell. . . ."

Then the odor was in Gefty's nostrils, too, and the back of his neck turned to ice as he recognized it. He glanced up at the ventilation outlet, looked back at Kerim.

He took her arm, said softly, "Come this way. Keep very quiet! I don't know how it happened, but the janandra's on the main deck now. That's what it smells like. The smell's coming through the ventilation system, so the thing's moving around in the port section. We'll go the other way."

Kerim whispered, "What will we do?"

"Get ourselves into spacesuits first, and then get Maulbow's control unit out of the ship. The janandra may be looking around for him. If it is, it won't bother us."

*H*e hadn't wanted to remind Kerim that, from what Maulbow said, there might be more than one reason for getting rid of the control unit as quickly as possible. But it had been constantly in the back of his mind; and twice, in the few minutes that passed after Maulbow's strange weapons were silenced, he had seen a momentary pale glare appear in the unquiet flow of darkness reflecting in the viewscreens. Gefty had said nothing, because if it was true that hostile forces were alert and searching for them here, it added to their immediate danger but not at all to the absolute need to free themselves from the inexorable rush of the Great Current before they were carried beyond hope of return to their civilization.

But those brief glimpses did add to the sense of urgency throbbing in Gefty's nerves, while events, and the equally hard necessity to avoid a fatally mistaken move in this welter of unknown factors, kept blocking him. Now the mysterious manner in which Maulbow's unpleasant traveling companion had appeared on the main deck made it impossible to do anything but keep Kerim at his side. If Maulbow was still capable of taking a hand in matters, there was no reasonably safe place to leave her aboard the *Queen*.

And Maulbow might be capable of it. Twice as they hurried up the narrow, angled passages along the *Queen's* curving hull towards an airseal leading to the next compartment, Gefty caught a trace of the ammonialike animal odor coming over the ventilating system. They reached the lock without incident; but then, as they came along the second deck hall to the ship's magazine, there was a sharp click in the stillness behind them. Its meaning was disconcertingly apparent. Gefty hesitated, turned Kerim into a side passage, guided her along it.

She looked up at his face. "It's following us?"

"Seems to be." No time for the spacesuits in the magazine now — something had just emerged from the air lock through which they had entered the second deck not many moments before. He helped the girl quickly down a section of ladderlike stairs to the airseal connecting the second deck with the storage, punched a wall button there. As the lock door opened, there was another noise from the passage they had just left, as if something had thudded briefly and heavily against one of the bulkheads. Kerim uttered a little gasp. Then they were in the lock, and Gefty slapped down two other buttons, stood watching the door behind them snap shut and, a few seconds later, the one on the far side open on the dark storage deck.

They scrambled down another twelve feet of ladder to the floor of a side passage, hearing the lock snap shut behind them. As it closed, they were in complete darkness. Gefty seized Kerim's arm, ran with her up the passage to the left, guiding himself with his fingertips on the left bulkhead. When they came to a corner, he turned her to the left again. A few seconds later, he pulled open a small door, bundled the girl through, came in himself, and shut the door to a narrow slit behind them.

Kerim whispered shakily, "What will we do now, Gefty?"

"Stay here for the moment. It'll look for us in the vault first."

And it should go to the storage vault first where it had been guarding Maulbow's machine, to hunt for them there. But it might not. Gefty eased the gun from his pocket on the far side of Kerim. Across the dark compartment was another door. They could retreat a little farther here if it became necessary — but not very much farther.

They waited in a silence that was complete except for their unsteady breathing and the distant, deep pulse of the *Queen's* throttled-down drives. He felt Kerim trembling against him. How did Maulbow's creature move through the airseal locks? The operating mechanisms were simple — a dog might have been taught to use them. But a dog had paws. . . .

There came the soft hiss of the opening lock, the faintest shimmer of light to the right of the passage mouth he was watching through the door. A heavy thump on the floor below the locks followed, then a hard click as the lock closed and complete darkness returned.

The silence resumed. Seconds dragged on. Gefty's imagination pictured the thing waiting, its great, wedge-shaped head raised as its senses probed the dark about it for a sign of the two human beings. Then a vague rushing noise began, growing louder as it approached the passage mouth, crossing it, receding rapidly again to the left.

Gefty let his breath out slowly, eased the door open and stood listening again. Abruptly, there was reflected light in the lock passage, coming now from the left. He said in a whisper,

"It's moving around in the main hall, Kerim. We can go on the other way now, but we'll have to be fast and keep quiet. I've thought of how we can get rid of that thing."

*T*he cargo lock on the storage deck had two inner doors. The one which opened into the side of the vault hall was built to allow passage of the largest chunks of freight the *Queen* was likely to be burdened with; it was almost thirty feet wide and twenty high. The second door was just large enough to let a man in a spacesuit climb in and out of the side of the lock without using the freight door. It opened on a tiny control cubicle from which the lock's mechanisms were operated during loading processes.

Gefty let Kerim and himself into the cubicle from one of the passages, steered the girl through the pitch blackness of the little room to the chair before the control panel and told her to sit down. He groped for a moment at the side of the panel, found a knob and twisted it.

There was a faint click. A scattering of pale lights appeared suddenly on the panel, a dark viewscreen, set at a tilt above them, reflecting their gleam.

Gefty explained in a low voice, "Left side of that screen covers the lock. Right one covers the big hall outside. No lights in either at the moment, so you don't see anything. Only way the cargo door to the hall can be opened or closed is with these switches right here. What I want to do is get the janandra into the lock, slam the door on it and lock down the control switches. Then we've got it trapped."

"But how are you going to get it to go in there?"

"No real problem — I'll be three jumps ahead of it. Then I duck back up into this cubicle, and lock both doors. And it'll be inside the lock. You have the picture now?"

Kerim said unsteadily, "I do. But it sounds awfully risky, Gefty."

"Well, I don't like it either," Gefty admitted. "So I'll start right now before I lose my nerve. As soon as I move out into the vault hall, the lighting will go on. That's automatic. You watch the right side of the screen. If you see the janandra coming before I do, yell as loud as you can."

He shifted the two inner door switches to the right. A red spark appeared in the dark viewscreen, high up near the center. A second red light showed on the cubicle bulkhead beside Gefty. Beneath it an oblong section of the bulkhead turned silently away on heavy hinges, became a door two feet in thickness, which stood jutting out at a right angle into the darkness of the cargo lock. A wave of cold air moved through it into the control cubicle.

On the screen, another red spark appeared beside the first one.

"Both doors are open now," Gefty murmured to the girl. "The janandra isn't in the vault hall or the lighting would have turned on, but it may have heard the door open and be on its way. So keep watching the screen."

"I certainly will!" she whispered shakily.

Gefty took an oversized wrench from the wall, climbed quickly and quietly down the three ladder steps to the floor of the lock, and walked across it to the sill of the giant freight door, which now had swung out and down into the vault hall, fitting itself into a depression of the flooring. He hesitated an instant on the sill, then stepped out into the big dark hall. Light filled it immediately in both directions.

He stood quiet, intent on the storage vault entrance far up the hall to his left. He could see the vault was open. The janandra might still be inside it. But the seconds passed, and the dark entrance remained silent and there was no suggestion of motion beyond it. Gefty glanced to the right, moved a dozen steps farther out into the hall, hefted the wrench and spun it through the air towards the ventilator frame on the opposite bulkhead.

The heavy tool clanged loudly against the frame, bounced off and thudded to the floor. Gefty started slowly over to it, heart pounding, with the vault entrance still at the edge of his vision.

Kerim's voice screamed, *"Gefty, it's —"*

He spun around, sprinted back to the cargo lock. The janandra had come silently out of the nearest side passage behind him, was approaching with the remembered oiling swiftness of motion, its great head lifted a yard from the floor. Gefty plunged through the lock, jumped for the top of the cubicle doorsteps, came stumbling into the cubicle. Kerim was on her feet, staring. He swung the cubicle door switch to the left, slapping it flat to the panel. The door snapped back into the wall behind him with a force that shook the floor.

On the screen, the janandra's thick, dark worm-shape was swinging around in the dim lock to regain the open hall. It had seen the trap. But the freight door switch went flat beside the other, and the freight door rose with massive swiftness. The heavy body smashed against it, went sliding back to the floor as the door slammed shut and the screen section showing the cargo lock turned dark.

"Got it — got it — got it!" Gefty heard himself whispering exultantly. He switched on the lock's interior lights.

Then he swore softly, and, beside him, Kerim sucked in her breath.

*T*he screen showed the janandra in violent but apparently purposeful motion inside the lock . . . and it was also apparent now that it was a more complexly constructed creature than the long worm-body and heavy head had indicated. The skin, to a distance of some eight feet back of the head, had spread out into a wide, flexible frill. From beneath the frill extended half a dozen jointed, bone-white arms, along with waving, ribbonlike appendages less easy to define. The thing was reared half up along the hall door, inspecting its surface with these members; then suddenly it flung itself around and flashed over to the outer lock door. Three arms shot out; wiry fingers caught the three spin-locks simultaneously, began to whirl them.

Gefty said, staring, "Kerim, it's going to . . ."

The janandra didn't. The motion checked suddenly, was reversed. The locks drew tight again. The janandra swung back from the door, lifting half its length upwards, big head weaving about as it inspected the tool racks overhead. An arm reached suddenly, snatched something from one of the racks. Then the thing turned again; and in the next instant its head filled the viewscreen. Kerim made a choked sound of fright, jerking back against Gefty. The bulging, metal-green eyes seemed to stare directly at him. And the screen went black.

Kerim whispered, "Wha . . . what happened, Gefty?"

Gefty swallowed, said, "It smashed the view pickup. Must have guessed we were watching and didn't like it. . . ." He added, "I was beginning to think Maulbow must be some kind of superman. But it wasn't any remote-control magic of his that let the janandra out of the vault, and opened the intership locks when it came up to the main deck and followed us down again. It was doing all that for itself. It's Maulbow's partner, not his pet. And it's probably got at least as good a brain as anyone else on board behind that ugly face."

Kerim moistened her lips. "Can it . . . could it get out again?"

"Into the ship?" Gefty shook his head decidedly. "Uh-uh. It could dump itself out on the other side — and it almost did before it realized where it was and what it was about to do. But the inner lock doors won't open until someone opens them right on this panel. No, the thing's safely trapped. On the other hand . . ."

On the other hand, Gefty realized that he wouldn't now be able to bring himself to eject the janandra out of the cargo lock and into the Great Current. Its intentions obviously hadn't been friendly, but its level of intelligence was as good as his own, and perhaps somewhat better;

and at present it was helpless. To dispose of it as he'd had in mind would therefore be the cold-blooded murder of an equal. But so long as that ugly and formidable shipmate of Maulbow's stayed in the cargo lock, the lock couldn't be used to get rid of the control unit in the vault.

A new solution presented itself while Gefty was making a rapid and rather desperate mental review of various heavy-duty tools which might be employed as weapons to force the janandra into submission and haul it off for confinement elsewhere in the ship. Not impossible, but a highly precarious and time-consuming operation at best. Then another thought occurred: the storage vault lay directly against the hull of the *Queen* —

How long to cut through the hull? The ship's mining equipment was on board, and the tools were self-powered. Climb into a spacesuit, empty the air from the entire storage deck, leaving the janandra imprisoned in the cargo lock ... with Maulbow incapacitated in sick bay, and Kerim back in the control compartment and also in a suit, for additional protection. Then cut ship's power to this deck to avoid complications with the *Queen's* involved circuitry and work under space conditions — half an hour if he hurried.

"Shouldn't take more than another ten minutes," he informed Kerim presently over the suit's intercom.

"I'm very glad to hear it, Gefty." She sounded shaky.

"Anything going on in the screens?" he asked.

She hesitated a little, said, "No. Not at the moment."

Gefty grunted, blinked sweat from his eyes, and took hold of the handgrips of the heavy mining cutter again, turning it nose down towards the vault floor. The guide light found the point he was working on, and the slice beam stabbed out, began nibbling delicately away to extend the curving line it had eaten through the

Queen's thick skin. He had drawn a twenty-five foot circle around Maulbow's battered control unit and the instruments attached to it, well outside the fragile-looking safety field. The circle was broken at four points where he would plant explosives. The explosives, going off together, should shatter the connecting links with the hull and throw the machine clear. If that didn't release them immediately from its influence, he would see what putting the *Queen's* drives into action would do.

"Gefty?" Kerim's voice asked.

"Uh-huh?"

He could hear her swallow over the intercom. "Those lights are back now."

"How many?"

"Two," Kerim said. "I *think* they're only two. They keep crossing back and forth in front of us." She laughed nervously. "It's idiotic, of course, but I do get the feeling they're looking at us."

Gefty said hesitantly, "Everything's set but I need another minute or two to get this last connection whittled down a little more. If I blow the charge too soon, it mightn't take the gadget clean out of the ship."

Kerim said, "I know. I'll just watch . . . they just disappeared again." Her voice changed. "Now there's something else."

"What's that?"

"You know you said to watch the cargo lock lights on the emergency panel."

"Yes."

"The outer lock door has just been opened."

"What!"

"It must have been. The light started blinking red just now as I was looking at it."

Gefty was silent a moment, his mind racing. Why would the janandra open the lock? From what Maulbow had said, it could live for a while without air, but it still could gain nothing but eventual death from leaving the ship —

Unless, Gefty thought, the janandra had become aware in some way that he was about to blow their machine out of the *Queen*. There were grappling lines in the cargo lock, and if four or five of those lines were slapped to the circular section of the hull he'd loosened . . .

"Kerim," he said.

"Yes?"

"I'm going to blow the deal right now. Got your suit snapped to the wall braces like I showed you?"

"Yes, Gefty." Her voice was faint but clear.

He turned the cutter away from the line it had dug, sent it rolling off towards the far wall. He hurried around the circle, checking the four charges, lumbered over to the vault passage, stopped just around the corner. He took the firing box from his suit.

"Ready, Kerim?" He opened the box.

"Ready. . . ."

"Here goes!" Gefty reached into the box, twisted the firing handle. Light flared in the vault. The deck shook below him. He came stumbling out from behind the wall.

Maulbow's machine and its stand of instruments had vanished. Where it had stood was a dark circular hole. Nothing else seemed to have happened. Gefty clumped hurriedly over to the mining cutter, swung it around, started more cautiously back towards the hole. He didn't have the faintest idea what would come next, but a definite possibility was that he would see the janandra's dark form flowing up over the rim of the hole. Letting it run into the cutter beam might be the best way to discourage it from reentering the *Queen.*

Instead, a dazzling brilliance suddenly blotted out everything. The cutter was plucked from Gefty's grasp; then he was picked up, suit and all, and slammed up towards the vault ceiling. He had a feeling that inaudible thunders were shaking the ship. He seemed to be rolling over and over along the ceiling. At last, the suit crashed into something which showed a total disinclination to yield, and Gefty blacked out.

*T*he left side of his face felt pushed out of shape; his left eye wasn't functioning too well, and there was a severe pulsing ache throughout the top of his head. But Gefty felt happy.

There were a few qualifying considerations.

"Of course," he pointed out to Kerim, "all we can really say immediately is that we're back in normspace and somewhere in the galaxy."

She smiled shakily. "Isn't that saying quite a lot, Gefty?"

"It's something." Gefty glanced around the instrument room. He had placed an emergency light on the console, but except for that, the control compartment was in darkness. The renewed battering the *Queen* had absorbed had knocked out the power in the forward section. The viewscreens were black, every instrument dead. But he'd seen the stars of normspace through the torn vault floor. It was something. . . .

"We might have the light that slugged us to thank for that," he said. "I'm not sure just what did happen there, but it could have been Maulbow's control unit it was attacking rather than the ship. Maulbow said the lights were sensitive to the unit. At any rate, we're here, and we're rid of the gadget — and of the janandra." He hesitated. "I just don't feel you should get your hopes too high. We may find out we're a very long way from the Hub."

Kerim's large eyes showed a degree of confidence which made him almost uncomfortable. "If we are," she said serenely, "you'll get us back somehow."

Gefty cleared his throat. "Well, we'll see. If the power shutoff is something the *Queen's* repair scanners can handle, the instruments will come back on any minute. Give the scanners ten minutes. If they haven't done it by that time, they can't do it and I'll have to play repairman. Then, with the instruments working, we can determine exactly where we are."

Unless, he told himself silently, they'd wound up in a distant cluster never penetrated by the Federation's mapping teams. And there was the other little question of where they now were in time. But Kerim looked rosy with relief, and those details could wait.

He took up another emergency light, switched it on and said, "I'll see how Maulbow is doing while we're waiting for power. If the first aid treatment has pulled him through so far, the autosurgeon probably can fix him up."

Kerim's face suddenly took on a guilty expression. "I forgot all about Mr. Maulbow!" She hesitated. "Should I come along?"

Gefty shook his head. "I won't need help. And if it's a case for the surgeon, you wouldn't like it. Those things work painlessly, but it gets to be a mess for a while."

He shut off the light again when he reached the sick bay which was running on its independent power system. As he opened the cabin door from the dispensary, carrying the autosurgeon, it became evident that Maulbow was still alive but that he might be in delirium. Gefty placed the surgeon on the table, went over to the bed and looked at Maulbow.

To the extent that the emergency treatment instruments' cautious restraints permitted, Maulbow was twisting slowly about on the bed. He was speaking in a low, rapid voice, his face distorted by emotion. The words were not slurred, but they were in a language Gefty didn't know. It seemed clear that Maulbow had reverted mentally to his own time, and for some seconds he remained unaware that Gefty had entered the room. Then, surprisingly, the slitted blue eyes opened wider and focused on Gefty's face. And Maulbow screamed with rage.

Gefty felt somewhat disconcerted. For the reason alone that he was under anesthetic, Maulbow should not have been conscious. But he was. The words were now ones Gefty could understand, and Maulbow was telling him things which would have been interesting enough under different circumstances. Gefty broke in as soon as he could.

"Look," he said quietly, "I'm trying to help you. I . . ."

Maulbow interrupted him in turn, not at all quietly. Gefty listened a moment longer, then shrugged. So Maulbow didn't like him. He couldn't say honestly that he'd ever liked Maulbow much, and what he was hearing made him like Maulbow considerably less. But he would keep the man from the future alive if he could.

He positioned the autosurgeon behind the head of the bed to allow the device to begin its analysis, stood back at its controls where he could both follow the progress it made and watch Maulbow without exciting him further by remaining within his range of vision. After a moment, the surgeon shut off the first-aid instruments and made unobtrusive use of a heavy tranquilizing drug. Then it waited.

Maulbow should have lapsed into passive somnolence thirty seconds afterwards. But the drug seemed to produce no more effect on him mentally than the preceding anesthetic. He raged and screeched on. Gefty watched him uneasily, knowing now that he was looking at insanity. There was nothing more he could do at the moment — the autosurgeon's decisions were safer than any nonprofessional's guesswork. And the surgeon continued to wait.

Then, abruptly, Maulbow died. The taut body slumped against the bed and the contorted features relaxed. The eyes remained half open; and when Gefty came around to the side of the bed, they still seemed to be looking up at him, but they no longer moved. A thin trickle of blood started from the side of the slack mouth and stopped again.

*T*he control compartment was still darkened and without power when Gefty returned to it. He told Kerim briefly what had happened, added, "I'm not at all sure now he was even human. I'd rather believe he wasn't."

"Why that, Gefty?" She was studying his expression soberly.

Gefty hesitated, said, "I thought at first he was furious because we'd upset his plans. But they weren't his plans . . . they were the janandra's. He wasn't exactly its servant. I suppose you'd have to say he was something like a pet animal."

Kerim said incredulously, "But that isn't possible! Think of how intelligently Mr. Maulbow . . ."

"He was following instructions," Gefty said. "The janandra let him know whatever it wanted done. He was following instructions again when he tried to kill me after I'd got away from the thing in the vault. The real brain around here was the janandra . . . and it was a real brain. With a little luck it would have had the ship."

Kerim smiled briefly. "You handled that big brain rather well, I think."

"I was the one who got lucky," Gefty said. "Anyway, where Maulbow came from, it's the janandra's kind that gives the orders. And the thing is, Maulbow liked it that way. He didn't want it to be different. When the light hit us, it killed the janandra on the outside of the ship. Maulbow felt it happen and it cracked him up. He wanted to kill us for it. But since he was helpless, he killed himself. He didn't want to be healed — not by us. At least, that's what it looks like."

He shrugged, checked his watch, climbed out of the chair. "Well," he said, "the ten minutes I gave the *Queen* to turn the power back on are up. Looks like the old girl couldn't do it. So I'll —"

The indirect lighting system in the instrument room went on silently. The emergency light flickered and went out. Gefty's head came around.

Kerim was staring past him at the screens, her face radiant.

"Oh, Gefty!" she cried softly. "Oh, Gefty! Our stars!"

"Green dot here is us," Gefty explained, somewhat hoarsely. He cleared his throat, went on, "Our true ship position, that is —" He stopped, realizing he was talking too much, almost babbling, in an attempt to take some of the tension out of the moment. The next few seconds might not tell them where they were, but it would show whether they had been carried beyond the regions of space charted by Federation instruments. Which would mean the difference between having a chance — whether a good chance or a bad one — of getting home eventually, and the alternative of being hopelessly lost.

There had been nothing recognizably familiar about the brilliantly dense star patterns in the viewscreens, but he gave no further thought to that. Unless the ship's exact position was known or one was on an established route, it was a waste of time looking for landmarks in a sizable cluster.

He turned on the basic star chart. Within the locator plate the green pinpoint of light reappeared, red-ringed and suspended now against the three-dimensional immensities of the Milky Way. It stayed still a moment, began a smooth drift towards Galactic East. Gefty let his breath out carefully. He sensed Kerim's eyes on him but kept his gaze fixed on the locator plate.

The green dot slowed, came to a stop. Gefty's finger tapped the same button four times. The big chart flicked out of existence, and in the plate three regional star maps appeared and vanished in quick succession behind it. The fourth map stayed. For a few seconds, the red-circled green spark was not visible here. Then it showed at the eastern margin of the map, came gliding forwards and to the left, slowed again and held steady. Now the star map began to glide through the locator plate, carrying the fixed green dot with it. It brought the dot up to dead center point in the locator plate and stopped.

Gefty slumped a little. He rubbed his hands slowly down his face and muttered a few words. Then he shook his head.

"Gefty," Kerim whispered, "what is it? Where are we?"

Gefty looked at her.

"After we got hauled into that time current," he said hoarsely, "I tried to find out which way in space we were headed. The direction indicators over there seemed to show we were trying to go everywhere at once. You remember Maulbow's control unit wasn't working right, needed adjustments. Well, all those little impulses must have pretty well canceled out because we weren't taken really far. In the last hour and a half we've covered roughly the distance the *Queen* could have gone on her own in, say, thirty days."

"Then where . . ."

"Home," Gefty said simply. "It's ridiculous! Other side of the Hub from where we started." He nodded at the plate. "Eastern Hub Quadrant. Section Six Eight. The G2 behind the green dot — that's the Evalee system. We could be putting down at Evalee Interstellar three hours from now if we wanted to."

Kerim was laughing and crying together. "Oh, Gefty! I knew you would . . ."

"A fat lot I had to do with it!" Gefty leaned forward suddenly, switched on the transmitter. "And now let's pick up a live newscast. There's something else I . . ."

His voice trailed off. The transmitter screen lit up with a blurred jumble of print, colors, a muttering of voices, music and noises. Gefty twisted a dial. The screen cleared, showed a newscast headline sheet. Gefty blinked at it, glanced sideways at Kerim, grimaced.

"The something else," he said, his voice a little strained, "was something I was also worried about. Looks like I was more or less right."

"Why, what's wrong?"

"Nothing really bad," Gefty assured her. He added, "I think. But take a look at the Federation dateline."

Kerim peered at the screen, frowned. "But . . ."

"Uh-huh."

"Why, that . . . that's almost . . ."

"That," Gefty said, "or rather *this* is the day after we started out from the Hub, headed roughly Galactic west. Three weeks ago. We'd be just past Miam." He knuckled his chin. "Interesting thought, isn't it?"

Kerim was silent for long seconds. "Then they . . . or we . . ."

"Oh, they're us, all right," Gefty said. "They'd have to be, wouldn't they?"

"I suppose so. It seems a little confusing. But I was thinking. If you send them a transmitter call . . ."

Gefty shook his head. "The *Queen's* transmitter isn't too hot, but it might push a call as far as Evalee. Then we could arrange for a Com-Web link-up there, and in another ten minutes or so . . . but I don't think we'd better."

"Why not?" Kerim demanded.

"Because we got through it all safely, so we're going to get through it safely. But if we receive that message now and never go on to Maulbow's moon . . . you see? There's no way of knowing just what would happen."

Kerim looked hesitant, frowned. "I suppose you're right," she agreed reluctantly at last. "So Mr. Maulbow will have to stay dead now. And that janandra." After a moment she added pensively, "Of course, they weren't really very nice —"

Gefty shivered. One of the things he'd learned from Maulbow's ravings was the real reason he and Kerim had been taken along on the trip. He didn't feel like telling Kerim about it just yet, but it had been solely because of Maulbow's concern for his master's creature comforts. The janandra could go for a long time without food, but after fasting for several years on the moon, a couple of snacks on the homeward run would have been highly welcome.

And the janandra was a gourmet. It much preferred, as Maulbow well knew, to have its snacks still wriggling-fresh as it started them down its gullet.

"No," Gefty said, "I couldn't call either of them really nice."